Acting Edition

I0591839

53% Of

by Steph Del Rosso

║SAMUEL FRENCH║

FOR PRODUCTION INQUIRIES

UNITED STATES AND CANADA
info@concordtheatricals.com
1-866-979-0447

UNITED KINGDOM AND EUROPE
licensing@concordtheatricals.co.uk
020-7054-7298

Each title is subject to availability from Concord Theatricals Corp., depending upon country of performance. Please be aware that *53% OF* may not be licensed by Concord Theatricals Corp. in your territory. Professional and amateur producers should contact the nearest Concord Theatricals Corp. office or licensing partner to verify availability.

No one shall make any changes in this title(s) for the purpose of production. No part of this book may be reproduced, stored in a retrieval system, scanned, uploaded, or transmitted in any form, by any means, now known or yet to be invented, including mechanical, electronic, digital, photocopying, recording, videotaping, or otherwise, without the prior written permission of the publisher. No one shall share this title(s), or any part of this title(s), through any social media or file hosting websites.

For all inquiries regarding motion picture, television, online/digital and other media rights, please contact Concord Theatricals Corp.

MUSIC AND THIRD-PARTY MATERIALS USE NOTE

Licensees are solely responsible for obtaining formal written permission from copyright owners to use copyrighted music and/or other copyrighted third-party materials (e.g. artworks, logos) in the performance of this play and are strongly cautioned to do so. If no such permission is obtained by the licensee, then the licensee must use only original music and materials that the licensee owns and controls. Licensees are solely responsible and liable for clearances of all third-party copyrighted materials, including without limitation music, and shall indemnify the copyright owners of the play(s) and their licensing agent, Concord Theatricals Corp., against any costs, expenses, losses and liabilities arising from the use of such copyrighted third-party materials by licensees. For music, please contact the appropriate music licensing authority in your territory for the rights to any incidental music.

IMPORTANT BILLING AND CREDIT REQUIREMENTS

If you have obtained performance rights to this title, please refer to your licensing agreement for important billing and credit requirements.

53% OF was first produced at the Second Stage Theater on June 28th, 2022. Carole Rothman was the President & Artistic Director; and Khady Kamara was the Executive Director. The performance was directed by Tiffany Nichole Greene and assistant directed by Myxolydia Tyler with sets by Emmie Finckel, costumes by Lux Haac, lighting design by Mextly Couzin, sound design by Jane Shaw, and dramaturgy by Christine Scarfuto. The Production Stage Manager was Kelly Hardy, and the Assistant Stage Manager was Chandalae Nyswonger. The cast was as follows:

LESLIE // LARRY // LUCY .... Marianna McClellan

DENISE // DEREK // DANA ....Anna Crivelli

SUE // STAN // SASHA.................................. Grace Rex

VICKY // VICTOR // VIVIAN..........................Cathryn Wake

PJ // RJ ....Eden Malyn

KJ ....Ayana Workman

Understudies: Sarah Goeke, Annie Young, and Kara F. Green.

53% OF was developed at the Ojai Playwrights Conference with Robert Egan as the Artistic Director/Producer. It was further developed at the Alliance Theatre and was the winner of the 2019/2020 Alliance/ Kendeda National Graduate Playwriting Competition.

CHARACTERS

LESLIE // LARRY // LUCY – White
DENISE // DEREK // DANA – White
SUE // STAN // SASHA – White
VICKY // VICTOR // VIVIAN – White
PJ // RJ – White
KJ – Black

The characters in Scenes One and Two are in their thirties to forties.
The characters in Scenes Three and Four are in their twenties to thirties.

SETTING

Scenes One and Two – The living room of a home in Bethlehem,
Pennsylvania.
Scene Three – An apartment in Brooklyn.
Scene Four – A bar in Harlem.

TIME

December 2016 – March 2017.

AUTHOR'S NOTES

In 2016, 53% of white women voted for Donald Trump.*
In 2020, 55% of white women voted for Donald Trump.*
While we're here:
56% of white women voted for Mitt Romney.*
53% of white women voted for John McCain.*
55% of white women voted for George W. Bush.*

/ indicates when the next line begins.
(words in parentheses) *are* unspoken.
[words in brackets] are spoken under the breath.
Caps in the Middle of a Sentence are meant for emphasis.
Things move fast. Periods at the end of a sentence are often the exception,
not the norm. Transitions are instantaneous. When one scene ends, the

---

* Sources found at the end of the text

next begins immediately, so an actor's character transformation must propel any transformation of the set or space.

No one is a caricature in this play. Embrace their full complexities. Embody them as earnestly as possible. And remember that the women in this play are very very very Nice to each other. Politeness can be weapon. Or a mask. Or a lot of things.

Scene One

(December 2016.)

(The living room of a house in Bethlehem, Pennsylvania.)

(Christmas decorations line the space.)

(It's cold outside.)

LESLIE. So I'm standing there, beneath this spotlight. And I'm kind of, you know, raised up

VICKY. Like you were levitating?

LESLIE. No no I was just higher than the rest of the crowd

DENISE. What were you wearing

LESLIE. Sorry?

DENISE. I can't tell you how many dreams I've had where I'm wearing my prom dress

VICKY. Once a prom queen always a, right?

SUE. It must be such a cherished memory for you that's SO nice

DENISE. Well it was the skinniest time in my life

  (Micro pause.)

SUE & VICKY. You're tiny; You look incredible; You're a stick [etc. etc.] /

LESLIE. Anyway, the dream

DENISE. Oh my goodness sorry Leslie!

LESLIE. Oh my goodness absolutely no apology necessary Denise! So I'm wearing – I don't actually remember what I'm wearing but I DO remember that I'm standing in front of this giant TV screen. And on the screen is this red bouncy ball.

SUE. *(...)* Like a, kid's toy?

LESLIE. No it's one of those balls that bounce around so you can follow the lyrics to a song. Because...

I'm singing karaoke! In my dream!

(This doesn't really get a response...)

I mean when's the last time I sang in public? The fourth grade caroling trip? Maybe? And here I am belting out Aretha Franklin

(There's her crowd.)

DENISE. I love Aretha.

(SUE tries to sing a song in the style of "Respect" by Aretha Franklin. She's not quite getting it.*)

SUE. Wait how does it go

(VICKY jumps in. She's actually kind of great.)

SUE. Look at you!

DENISE. *(Jealous...)* I had no idea you were a singer.

SUE. Go Vicky!

---

* A license to produce *53% Of* does not include a performance license for any third-party or copyrighted music. Licensees should create an original composition or use music in the public domain. For further information, please see the Music and Third-Party Materials Use Note on page iii.

VICKY. Ladies this is what happens when I drink red wine in the afternoon

DENISE. Sue, you sure you don't want any?

SUE. Oh I'm fine, I'm fine

LESLIE. *(Come on guys.)* So, um, ladies

The craziest thing about this dream was: Guess who I was singing to? Guess who I was serenading?

(Is this question rhetorical?)

(What's going on here?)

*(***LESLIE*** *is really bad at telling stories in public.)*

It was – I was singing to

HIM!

VICKY & SUE & DENISE. Oooh, wow, oh my goodness etc.

LESLIE. *(Getting a little lost in it...)* In his suit, and his bright red tie! Swaying to the music and looking just so, Stately. You know? And he was staring at me, he was Staring Square At Me and then he was climbing – because the place where I was singing was actually really high off the ground, suspended in air maybe? It was like when you're on a plane, and you're peering down at tiny toy cars and tiny toy people except he wasn't tiny and he wasn't made of plastic: He Was Real, sweating through his shirt, using his muscles, climbing and climbing and climbing and getting closer and closer and closer, not taking his eyes off me

(Maybe she's finally captured the room's attention at this point.)

And then I woke up.

DENISE. *(That's it?)* Oh.

LESLIE. But that's not all. Because when I woke up, do you know what I did? I started belly laughing, like real in my ribs laughing

SUE. *(...)* Were you alright

LESLIE. Oh my goodness I was beyond alright, Sue! I was basically euphoric because it hit me: This was a sign. This dream was telling me something.

> *(She thinks they know.)*

> *(They don't.)*

VICKY. *(...)* What was it telling you

LESLIE. That

I should be the one to introduce him. When he comes. To the school.

> *(Energy shift.)*

DENISE. *(...)* I'm a little lost

VICKY. Yeah I don't get it.

LESLIE. It felt like a premonition /

SUE. Um, I'm not super comfortable with that word

LESLIE. Oh, I'm / sorry

SUE. I'd just rather not [say it.] Makes me think of, potions and witches and blegh /

LESLIE. Oh. Yikes. Sure. Um

I guess I'm just saying, the dream was a personal reminder for me, that I've been devoted to this campaign and to this mission and to this person / for

VICKY. We're all devoted

SUE. We're all incredibly devoted

LESLIE. Right! RIGHT! You are each super devoted individually. It was just a wake-up call – HA literally a wake-up call, for myself, about my own. Commitment

> *(Awkward beat.)*

> *(This didn't exactly play as she had planned...)*

DENISE. That's really sweet, Leslie. Thank you for sharing your story.

LESLIE. *(...)* No problem

DENISE. And thank you for bringing up a crucial question that I know is on a lot of our minds, am I right ladies? Who will introduce him?

VICKY. Well I just want to say that my kids would be Thrilled. Did I tell you that the twins dressed up like him? For Halloween? With the red hats and everything? Did I show you the photo / *(?)*

DENISE. You did Vicky, yes.

SUE. Personally I feel a bit of a spiritual calling to him and I think that's, I think that's powerful

LESLIE. Yes. Definitely. Powerful

But Sue don't forget that he himself is not, you know

SUE. What?

LESLIE. ...Religious

SUE. *(...)* Okay

LESLIE. So we don't want to,

scare him

SUE. *(Offended.)* UM

DENISE. What she means is you may not be the ideal spokeswoman for this particular task. Even though there are plenty of other tasks you could really shine at

SUE. You, think so?

DENISE. Absolutely!

I'd just like to throw my hat in the ring and remind you all that I feel a Deep kinship with his daughter. I mean, a businesswoman, an author, And a mom? She does it all, and I really see myself in her ability to, balance – you all know how important balance is for me. And I promise you, I will channel that, channel Her in a speech that will certainly make our beloved Bethlehem community proud.

> (**SUE** *and* **VICKY** *seem begrudgingly convinced. It's a good argument.*)

> (**LESLIE** *isn't buying it.*)

LESLIE. I tried on her heels today.

DENISE. Did you?

LESLIE. They were at Macy's, yeah, I tried them on.

DENISE. That's so funny I didn't think that was your style.

VICKY. Oh kay. How about: whoever wants to introduce him, raise your hand

> (*Everyone raises her hand.*)

> (*And then* **DENISE** *tightly smiles at* **SUE**.)

> (**SUE** *brings her hand down.*)

> (**DENISE** *tightly smiles at* **VICKY** *and* **LESLIE**.)

> (*Their hands remain where they are.*)

DENISE. (*Haha!*) Vicky, don't you get stage fright?

VICKY. *(Haha!)* No not at all

DENISE. I could've sworn, at the Harvest Festival...

SUE. That's true, when you were supposed to announce the, what was it?

DENISE. The pumpkin decorating contest winners

LESLIE. Right, the pumpkins. You did turn a little /

DENISE. (Green)

VICKY. I had a fever

DENISE. It's completely okay if you don't like speaking in public

VICKY. I had a fever

DENISE. No judgment here!

VICKY. Okay I was a little. Outside my comfort zone.

DENISE. And we're SO proud of you for getting uncomfortable like that!

But I'm thinking, I mean I don't know what you're thinking, but I'm thinking the stakes for this are pretty high. Plus, your AMAZING talents with children would be perfectly suited for handling the crowd, making sure the kids are quiet, etc. etc.

> *(VICKY puts her hand down.)*
>
> *(LESLIE still has her hand up.)*
>
> *(DENISE still has her hand up.)*
>
> *(They look at each other.)*
>
> *(Tight smiles. Maybe some forced laughter.)*
>
> *(It's almost like a game of chicken: who will drop her hand first?)*

(But their hands remain raised.)

(The doorbell rings.)

LESLIE. Just a second!

(Leslie goes to get the door.)

(Does she keep her hand raised as she goes?)

(The ladies mill about.)

*(**DENISE** looks pissed.)*

*(When **LESLIE** returns, **PJ** is at her side.)*

*(**PJ** is wearing a sweatshirt.)*

*(**PJ** is wearing a sweatshirt with a large Confederate flag stretched across it.)*

(Everyone notices and no one wants to notice.)

Ladies this is /

PJ. PJ. Hi, I'm PJ

...

...

...

SUE. Welcome!

*(The women stare at **PJ**.)*

*(**PJ** stares back.)*

PJ. I brought Green Stuff.

LESLIE. *(...)* Pardon?

PJ. I wasn't sure if this was a potluck or, you know, "Never come empty-handed" so, Green Stuff

> (**PJ** *indicates the large bowl she's holding.*)
>
> (*Something gooey is inside it.*)
>
> (*It's green.*)
>
> (*Brief pause.*)

DENISE. Oh that's really kind of you

VICKY. Super kind

SUE. So thoughtful

LESLIE. (*Too excitedly.*) YUM!

> (**LESLIE** *takes the Green Stuff from* **PJ** *with zero intention of serving it.*)

DENISE. (*A challenge.*) Leslie, should we get some bowls?

LESLIE. Oh. Are we all hungry, now?

VICKY. (It *is* 4:30)

LESLIE. (*Stung.*) I'm sorry the spinach pies should only be another, half hour or so - they were a little (frozen) so I had / to

PJ. Green Stuff's ready to serve!

DENISE. PJ saves the day! Right ladies?

SUE. I guess I could have, a little nibble

VICKY. (...) Sounds great

LESLIE. ...Great! Let me just /

PJ. I'll help!

> (**PJ** *and* **LESLIE** *head to the kitchen.*)

(**DENISE**, **VICKY**, *and* **SUE** *watch them go, all smiles.*)

(*Immediately once they've disappeared: gossip mode.*)

(*This moves fast.*)

DENISE. *(??)* Who in the world /

VICKY. "PJ"? What kind of name / is

SUE. Did Leslie tell you guys she was bringing a new member in/to

DENISE & VICKY. No

SUE. Okay so it's not just me

VICKY. Did she recently move here?

DENISE. I've never seen her in my life

VICKY. So maybe she's from. Nearby

SUE. What do you mean Nearby

VICKY. I don't know, Wind Gap?

　　　　(The women cringe.)

　Easton?

　　　　(The women cringe.)

DENISE. Or probably

　Stockertown

SUE. Oh dear

VICKY. *(Ugh!)* Oh god you think she's from Stockertown?

SUE. Did you see her

　　　[sweatshirt.]

VICKY. Her what?

SUE. Her – Come on you know what I'm talking about

DENISE. Yes we obviously know what you're talking about

SUE. So what exactly should we

> Do

> about that

VICKY. There's isn't anything we can Do

DENISE. Ask her to take it off?

VICKY. What if she's not wearing anything underneath it?

DENISE. *(Haha!)* Ew

VICKY. *(Haha!)* Ew

SUE. I think it's a little weird to, you know,

DENISE. Display that on your chest? I agree

VICKY. I think it's a little weird that we're supposed to be all la dee da about this stranger

SUE. Do you think Leslie has one?

VICKY. Has one what

SUE. Do you think Leslie has a / [sweatshirt.]

> *(But LESLIE and PJ burst back into the room.)*

LESLIE. *(Renewed peppiness.)* Oh KAY!

PJ. Here we GO!

LESLIE. Bon Appetit ladies!

> *(LESLIE and PJ pass out the bowls.)*

VICKY. Looks yummy!

> *(It doesn't.)*

DENISE. Are these pineapple chunks by chance?

PJ. That's crushed pineapple in heavy syrup, lime Jell-O, whipped cream, cream cheese, and marshmallows

SUE. Sounds

Wow

DENISE. Oh NO

LESLIE. What's wrong?

DENISE. I'm allergic to pineapple! I am SO sorry PJ

> (*PJ shrugs. Takes* DENISE*'s bowl from her. Pours it into her own bowl.*)

> (LESLIE *takes a teeny tiny bite. Scrunches up her face a bit too obviously.*)

> (VICKY *moves her spoon around and around in her bowl, smooshing the contents so they look smaller.*)

> (SUE *is actually kind of into it. She eats happily.*)

> (PJ *devours her two servings.*)

> (DENISE *watches her do this. She's grossed out.*)

(*To* PJ.) I'm Denise, by the way. And that's Vicky, and that's Sue.

LESLIE. (*A bad joke.*) And I'm Leslie! But you know that already.

DENISE. Yeah, how did you say you two know each other?

PJ. Facebook.

LESLIE. I posted on the Northampton County Supporters Page. Thought it might be nice to expand our group a little, to towns in the area. Towns where he isn't visiting schools or doing victory speeches.

DENISE. Expand, huh. Call me crazy but I don't think that's something we all agreed to?

LESLIE. Well I just figured, all hands on deck, right? The more the merrier.

VICKY. *(Trying...)* That's. Very generous of you

PJ. That's what I thought. I said to myself, that Leslie sounds pretty decent. And I'd kill to meet him, even just to touch him HA!

I mean shake his hand, salute him, whatever. Tell him how excited I am. Super excited. FIRED UP!

So I thought, why not drive over to Bethlehem and check out what this Women for Freedom and Family Group is up to?

DENISE. Sure. Why not?

> *(The women consider* **PJ.***)*

> *(All except* **LESLIE** *judge her.)*

SUE. Can I just say – I don't really *understand* Facebook.

DENISE. What's there to not understand?

SUE. How do they know I shop at Giant? The people who – the computer programmers or [whatever.] The ads running up and down the side are always for Giant.

VICKY. It's something in the system – it's a formula

LESLIE. I kind of, Love Facebook. I mean, online things are. Big. Right? Things are. Wider. World Wide Web, ha!

> **(PJ** *laughs. No one else does.)*

LESLIE. *(Maybe this will explain it:)* I don't know about you all but, being on Facebook gives me a little shiver like a little tingly feeling on my, on my scalp

DENISE. *(...?)* Your scalp

LESLIE. And also on my lower back

VICKY. *(...)* Okay

LESLIE. Being in those Facebook groups makes me feel like I'm, like I'm

(cheating on Larry!)

yeah

with some strange man I met at a rest-stop on I-70 who's a little sweaty a little *thick* you know like he could crush you like he could lie on top of you and smother you and sometimes that's what you want that's exactly what you want more than anything in the world

　　(Realizing.)

Sorry I'm getting a little [personal.]

PJ. I'm with you, Leslie. I'm all about Facebook. No one's telling you what you're supposed to say, no walking on eggshells. Because I have no time for eggshells, all I have time for is free speech you know?

　　　　(VICKY, SUE, *and* **DENISE** *look at* **PJ***'s sweatshirt.)*

　　　　(Look away.)

　　　　(LESLIE *remains focused on her Green Stuff.)*

SUE. You guys sound just like Stan – *(To* PJ.*)* my husband. He loves the internet. Spends hours and hours in the den, typing away. Gets so wrapped up in whatever it is that he's doing he forgets to turn the lamp on! And I see him in there, his face lit up by that blue light from the screen and I tell him, "Stan you're gonna ruin your eyes!" and he says,

"Get out of here Sue! Get out of my sight!"

Ha ha

He's only kidding ha ha

(Awkward.)

Do you have a, special someone, PJ?

PJ. A what?

VICKY. Do you have a husband

PJ. Oh. Yup. RJ

LESLIE. *(!)* Larry's actually hosting an inauguration party next month! Maybe RJ could join

DENISE. *(Uh...)* I didn't hear about this

LESLIE. It's just a, husband thing

"Boys only no girls allowed"

> *(**DENISE** begins idly running her hand up and down **LESLIE**'s mantle.)*

PJ. Where's it at?

LESLIE. Right here at our place!

*(To **DENISE**.)* And Derek is of course welcome

> *(**DENISE**'s hand is now covered with dust from **LESLIE**'s mantle. She tries to wipe it off, looking displeased.)*

> *(**LESLIE** notices. Everyone notices.)*

> *(Awkward. Can **LESLIE** salvage this?)*

We recently had to. Let Paola go

PJ. Let who what?

LESLIE. Paola. Our housekeeper.

VICKY. Was she stealing from you?

LESLIE. No no I just started to

Question her

work ethic.

>*(Weird beat. What is* **LESLIE** *talking about? Then:)*

DENISE. Oh I almost forgot to tell you all: we finished the basement!

VICKY. Congrats!

SUE. Wow!

DENISE. You ladies *must* come over soon. We found this absolutely gorgeous leather lounge chair collection and Derek even installed...a bar. We could make margaritas!

SUE. *(If only...)* How fun

DENISE. I love your home Leslie I really do love it

LESLIE. Thank you!

DENISE. It's just nice to have room to, you know, stretch out.

>*(This is a subtle dig at* **LESLIE***'s house.)*

>*(The women clock this.)*

LESLIE. Of course.

>*(Tactic shift:)* Does Brianne ever hang out in the basement?

DENISE. From time to time, yes.

LESLIE. I hope you're keeping an eye on her down there.

DENISE. What do you mean?

LESLIE. Well isn't that where that awful thing happened with Cammie Barclay? Wasn't that in someone's basement?

DENISE. *(Um!)* Brianne is nothing like Cammie Barclay

SUE. Is she really saying it was Tommy Nicklesworth? Because I just don't – I just can't picture –

LESLIE. I know, he is such a nice boy. Extremely polite

SUE. Two weeks ago he shoveled my front drive

VICKY. The important thing to remember is that he didn't force her to, [have sex.] you know

He just forced her to...

DENISE. Pleasure him

SUE. Okay we don't have to get into all the / [details.]

LESLIE. Allegedly

VICKY. Allegedly, yes. But see, if they didn't actually, you know, [have sex] then that's not, like Technically that's not

[assault]

Right?

It's almost like saying, if Victor had some other woman do, That to him, well, it wouldn't be cheating. Not unless they actually, you know

So, maybe the same thing applies. Maybe it's not, Technically Speaking [assault]

SUE. Right right I agree

DENISE. I heard Cammie's saying this has happened *before*

LESLIE. So why didn't she speak up? Why didn't she come forward earlier if it happened to her earlier?

SUE. *(Genuinely concerned.)* How did we raise our daughters to be liars?

LESLIE & DENISE. My daughter is not a liar

SUE. No no I know, Madison and Brianne are great girls, / but

VICKY. These ladies need to realize that if they want people to believe them, they have to / record things

DENISE. Record things, right. They need evidence just like / anyone else needs evidence

VICKY & SUE. Just like anyone else needs evidence, that's right; Just like anyone else, uh huh [etc.]

LESLIE. Larry has this theory: Larry told me that you can tell when someone's lying by paying attention to where they're looking, just before they speak. And if they look to the left, then they're activating the creative side of their brain, and that means they're lying.

So I've been paying attention to that, lately. People who look to the left. Before they speak

SUE. *(...)* Wow

VICKY. *(...)* Huh.

DENISE. *(...)* That's fascinating

PJ. Can someone catch me up on what exactly you all have been Working On today?

DENISE. *(Not actually apologetic.)* Looks like we're boring PJ

SUE. *(Loaded.)* Maybe she wants to talk about, other things

DENISE. *(Loaded.)* Yeah. Like, fashion.

PJ. *(Big smile?)* Just eager to accomplish something instead of chit-chatting about, basements.

LESLIE. Um, ladies, why don't we fill her in

DENISE & VICKY. We were just deciding /

DENISE. Oh my goodness so sorry to interrupt Vicky!

VICKY. Go right ahead Denise!

DENISE. No really Vicky you go!

VICKY. No no after you!

DENISE. Thank you!

We were just deciding who will introduce him. You know, invite him up to the podium

LESLIE. Either, me or Denise

DENISE. Me or Leslie

> *(Tight smiles.)*

PJ. So what else is going to happen? Like, after the intro. Aren't we supposed to put on a show for him? Hold an assembly?

> *(Brief brief beat.)*

> *(The women hadn't considered this. Then:)*

DENISE. We can have concert band perform.

VICKY. ...They'll be in Miami

DENISE. *(!)* The band trip is the same week he comes?

LESLIE. That is a *major* school board oversight

SUE. Jacob will be heartbroken!

VICKY. *(An idea!)* What about if the kids do a skit. A show and tell.

DENISE. *(Skeptical.)* Show and tell?

VICKY. So they can SHOW him what they love about his plans for our country! Can someone be the secretary?

SUE. I can!

VICKY. My vision is that every kid has a little moment in the spotlight where they tell a personal story and then – Sue are you writing this down?

SUE. Oh shoot, I didn't know we / were

VICKY. If you're going to be the secretary / then

SUE. I'm sorry let / me

> (**SUE** *scrambles to find something to write on in* **LESLIE***'s living room.*)

LESLIE. I think the first line should be,

"I'm really sad."

SUE. *(Writing.)* "I'm really sad," okay

DENISE. Hang on – aren't we going for more of a, celebratory mood?

LESLIE. Well they Start sad because it's Before he won / but then we move to After he's won and they're –

SUE. Can you guys – sorry – Can you guys talk a little slower? I'm not getting this all down

VICKY. Sue, come on

PJ. Why don't we just record it? On someone's phone or something. Won't that be faster?

SUE. I don't want this going on YouTube

PJ. It's not going on YouTube

LESLIE. But how would we record it unless we have /

VICKY. *(An idea!!!!)* A mini tripod!!!

...

Sorry! HaHA sorry to get all *(An excited sound.)* It was a present from Victor, so sweet right? We'd just been kind of um butting heads lately and blah blah blah boring! But he knows I love selfies and the group shots with the kids so one morning he handed me this box from Best Buy and...

> *(**VICKY** rifles in her purse, pulls out a mini tripod for an iPhone.)*

Ta da!

> *(Brief beat.)*

SUE. Wow Victor is so good to you

> *(**VICKY** sets up the tripod and puts her phone inside it as she speaks the following:)*

VICKY. Now go stand over there by that lamp so you'll all be in the –

You too Sue! All hands on deck, right? Leslie you can clean later, we'll help! Go ahead and – great. Sue a little to the left? We can't see you! And PJ a little to the – yes. And Denise why don't you stand next to –

> *(**DENISE** gives **VICKY** a look as she settles to the side with a glass of wine. She's sitting this one out.)*

Nevermind – that's perfect. Stay there, don't move. Let me just press –

> *(**VICKY** presses record.)*

> *(She joins the others.)*

> *(They stand there, staring at the iPhone.)*

> *(Frozen.)*

(They stand there.)

(And then suddenly:)

PJ. *(Weird little kid voice.)* I'm really sad you guys!

VICKY. Okay is that...?

DENISE. What are you...?

PJ. *(Weird little kid voice.)* I'm really sad you guys!

SUE. Should I be writing this down?

LESLIE. No Sue, we're recording now

SUE. Oh right

LESLIE. *(Little kid voice.)* Why are you sad, PJ?

> *(The little kid voices continue throughout the following:)*

PJ. Because my mommy and my daddy had been working super duper hard at their job in the steel mill. But then one day the mill went POOF. We looked outside and there was a hole where the mill used to be. Just holes and holes and holes, like the moon. And it felt like the moon too cuz there were aliens, I mean ILLEGAL aliens, all over the place! It was like an, Infestation – everywhere we turned: Strangers! And not just any strangers but Dangerous ones, out to get us, out to take over our –

> *(**VICKY** nudges **SUE** to go next.)*

SUE. I'm sad too PJ!

PJ. Oh no! You are??

SUE. Um yes – Yes I am! Because

Because

Children are dying. Okay? Sixty-Two Million children – one fifth of our population – have been exterminated!

Sixty-two million children who – who, *(Remembering character.)* I'll never get to meet, who I'll never get to play with on the playground! All because there are people who want to Murder an innocent human life /

VICKY. But my mommy and daddy told me that there's someone out there who's gonna fix all these bad things! That starting next year, there's someone who's gonna save all the babies and kick out all the evil criminals! Who's gonna clean the scary cities and bring back all the jobs!

PJ. Is that true?

SUE. Pretty please say it is!

DENISE. *(Eye roll.)* Can we move this along?

LESLIE. *(Deep voice.)* She is absolutely correct.

> *(The women look expectantly at **LESLIE**.)*

DENISE. What in / the

LESLIE. *(Stronger deep voice.)* I'm here! I've arrived!

And I have all the answers!

And all the ideas!

And ALL THE POWER

PJ. Yes / you do!

LESLIE. *(Full-on scary man's voice.)* LISTEN okay? Listen to me Do NOT interRUPT ME

I have many, many friends. And I have many, many supporters. And they're fantastic people. They're all fantastic people. But they've had to deal with some very bad things, very very bad things. And some very unfair things, very very unfair. So now they need ME. Because I'm gonna bring people to their feet, to their knees. I'm gonna have crowds cheering, screaming, begging for more. I'm gonna go down in the history books, believe me. And it's gonna be beautiful, absolutely beautiful. Because I am the world's greatest

LESLIE. I am untouchable

I am immortal

I am almighty

And I can do anything! They let me do ANYTHING!

I CAN DO ANYTHING!

> (**LESLIE** *soaks up all that imagined male power.*)
>
> (*It's terrifying.*)
>
> (*And then, she grabs the barely-eaten bowls of green stuff, sticks her hand inside them, and hurls a fistful of green stuff at* **SUE.**)
>
> (**PJ** *is delighted by this. Does she cheer a little?* **SUE** *notices.*)
>
> (*Then.*)
>
> (*An odd moment.*)
>
> (**LESLIE** *has no idea what came over her.*)
>
> (*Their regular voices return.*)

Let me get a /

PJ. There are some napkins / right [here.]

LESLIE. Great great thanks

VICKY. I hope that doesn't stain

DENISE. It looks like it stains

VICKY. Well

LESLIE. Whoops

VICKY. Sue, are you alright?

(**SUE** *is not alright.*)

(*She's upset. She's breathing heavily.*)

SUE. I'm fine

VICKY. Are you

sure

SUE. I'm fine

DENISE. She doesn't look /

SUE. I'm Fine

VICKY. Okay, okay

SUE. I just, I just

I

(*A blurt out.*) PJ where did you get that?

(*The women look at* **SUE**. *They did not expect this from her.*)

(*They look at* **PJ**.)

PJ. Get what.

SUE. That

You know

PJ. No I don't know

SUE. Where did you

get

your

Sweatshirt

LESLIE. (Sue what are you /)

PJ. At a store.

SUE. Okay. Sure. But I don't understand

Why

you're wearing it. Here.

VICKY. Ladies why don't / we

PJ. Because it has spiritual significance.

SUE. *(What does she say to that?)* Okay

Well...

PJ. This here is the blood of Christ

And the white border is God keeping us safe

And the blue X is Saint Anthony

DENISE. *(Skeptical.)* Saint Anthony?

PJ. The Saint of Lost Things

LESLIE. That's very interesting. Thank you / for

DENISE. So you're honoring The Saint of Lost Things?

PJ. That's right

DENISE. And what does that mean?

PJ. It means we're in danger

LESLIE. Well maybe that's something we can all agree / on

DENISE. I don't feel like I'm in danger

PJ. Then I don't think you're paying attention

DENISE. Wow, okay

PJ. The world's changing. Things are moving fast fast fast

VICKY. (She's right about that)

PJ. If we don't take a stand, if we don't remind people that we are Staying Put, then we're gonna get swept away

DENISE. So it's what, Heritage Not Hate, right? That's what people say?

LESLIE. Well she's allowed to honor her heri/tage

PJ. This isn't just about heritage. This is about truth. This is about claiming our truth.

I refuse to apologize for taking up space. I refuse to roll over while my children inherit a world where they're tormented, and denied success. I refuse to let everything that generations of my family earned just, shrivel up and perish.

This means we are not putting up with any of that. This means we deserve to be here – deserve to Thrive here! – and no one can compromise our thriving.

This is about hope. This is about choosing hope.

> *(Are the women a little struck by these words?)*

> *(But then.)*

DENISE. But it's also about

Something else

PJ. And what is that Something Else?

DENISE. *(Oh please.)* Come on

PJ. Really, why don't you spell it out for me?

LESLIE. I think we've had enough / of

DENISE. A lot of people look at that, and then look at you, and then put two and two together and think that you're,

That you're

> *(Even for **DENISE**, this is hard to bring into the room.)*

DENISE. Racist

> *(The word leaves a bad taste in everyone's mouth.)*

PJ. What did you just say?

VICKY. Uh, Denise /

LESLIE. *(Tight smile.)* She is our guest

DENISE. *(Sue me.)* I'm just making an observation

PJ. You don't know me

DENISE. Well first impressions are very important.

LESLIE. *(To* **DENISE.***)* We went to high school together! I know that You're not racist, and you know that *I'm* not racist /, so why would I bring

VICKY. I'm not a racist

And neither is Victor

DENISE. What does Victor have to do with this?

VICKY. Well he also has, um

one of those

DENISE. *(!)* He has a sweatshirt?

VICKY. No no no not a [sweatshirt.]

But just a little pin

PJ. See? Your husband's not a racist, just like I'm not a racist /

SUE. Can we stop using that word?

PJ. Or a homophobe. Or any of that stuff. The way I see it is: all those people have their rights now. Great. Woo hoo. So move on. You know? Let's get the actual show on the road

LESLIE. It's true, there is Way too much attention on all /
that

PJ. Other stuff, right?

DENISE. What do the stars represent?

PJ. The what

DENISE. The stars? *(She points.)*

You didn't mention

PJ. *(A quick lie.)* God's hands.

DENISE. *(Skeptical.)* God's hands?

PJ. God's hands

VICKY. Okay God's hands

> *(***DENISE** *considers* **PJ.***)*

DENISE. I don't like labels, I hate labels. But I have core
values. I have core moral values. And my values are not

That

PJ. What

DENISE. Are not

You

PJ. *(Offended.)* What?

VICKY. (Um, ladies)

DENISE. I'm not That

I'm not

You

SUE. Oh dear

PJ. Excuse me?

DENISE. *(Real vitriol.)* I'm not That I'm not You I'm not
You I am not

LESLIE. Ladies please

DENISE. I'm not I'm not I am Not

  I am Not You

Scene Two

(January 2017.)

(We're still in **LESLIE***'s living room. But this time, the women aren't the women anymore.)*

(The women are their husbands.)

(And the Christmas decorations are gone.)

(And they're drinking Scotch instead of wine.)

*(***LESLIE***, who is now* **LARRY***, is fiddling with a TV remote.)*

(We can't see the TV, but they can. And something's not working.)

LARRY. Shhhhhit

VICTOR. Are you serious Larry

LARRY. It's something with the Roku and the router

DEREK. You've got to get Apple TV, man

LARRY. Maybe if I reset /

RJ. We're missing it

LARRY. It doesn't start right on time

RJ. It's the inauguration, of course it starts on time

LARRY. But he's not swearing in yet

RJ. The swearing in is the first thing he does

LARRY. No, people sing the anthem and the Rockettes come out and dance

RJ. *(You idiot.)* The Rockettes are later

DEREK. You guys should see my basement, I've got a whole consul down there. And a bar. Denise has been making margaritas

VICTOR. (Should've met at your place)

LARRY. *(Re: the TV.)* Oh, oh – here it is. Here it is!

VICTOR. Nice

DEREK. Finally

RJ. *(Re: the TV.)* What's this?

VICTOR. I dunno, some choir

STAN. *(Eye roll.)* It's the Mormon Tabernacle Choir. Sue's obsessed with them

VICTOR. Is Sue...Mormon?

STAN. No she just loves anything that has to do with church

LARRY. See? We missed nothing.

> *(The men sip their Scotch.)*

> *(They idly look at the TV.)*

VICTOR. *(To LARRY.)* So were you gonna finish telling us about Maria, or...

LARRY. Who?

VICTOR. Your cleaning lady

LARRY. *(Come on.)* Her name's Paola

VICTOR. *(What?)* Okay. Paola. Kind of sounds like Maria

So you just flat-out denied it to Leslie?

LARRY. Yup. I said, Leslie, baby, love of my life: I have zero idea what you're talking about. I don't even speak Spanish

DEREK. Didn't you say she was Brazilian?

LARRY. *(Your point?)* Yeah?

DEREK. They don't speak Spanish in Brazil. They speak Portuguese

LARRY. I don't speak Portuguese either so, story still stands.

Anyway, Leslie starts crying,

RJ. Uh oh

LARRY. No no – that's when I realize: everything is going to be fine. Because if she's crying, she's vulnerable. I touch her, anywhere, hipbone, elbow / and she's like, jelly

DEREK. *(Psh.)* Elbow?

VICTOR. What do you mean by jelly

LARRY. You know what I mean by jelly

VICTOR. If I'm gonna be precise about it, twenty-five percent of the time, Vicky's still got it. But the rest of the time, I'm lying there, eyes closed, trying to pretend she's, you know, Trina Tippett

LARRY. Trina Tippett ho-ly SHIT

VICTOR. Right?

RJ. Who's this?

STAN. When we were all in high school, cheerleader, huge *(Tits gesture.)*

VICTOR. *(Wistfully.)* She was a queen

LARRY. *(Wistfully.)* She was a skank

VICTOR. Queen Skank

DEREK. Guys, come on. She has a family now

LARRY. *(So?)* Okay

VICTOR. Where?

DEREK. Married a marine. Stationed in Hawaii

VICTOR. No shit. I'm picturing her in one of those grass, you know, with the coconut bra or whatever. Doing the luau

DEREK. Hula

VICTOR. No I'm pretty sure it's luau

RJ. So who's Trina Tippett 2017?

> *(Slight slight hesitation from the men.)*

> *(Then.)*

VICTOR. Uh

That'd probably be Cammie Barclay

RJ. Yeah? What's she like?

LARRY. *(To* **VICTOR.***)* You think so? I don't know. Cammie doesn't have a girl-next-door, vibe. She's a little *(A gesture/sound implying "dirty".)*

STAN. What about Lisa Goldwater

LARRY. That the gymnast?

STAN. Uh huh

VICTOR. Who?

LARRY. The gymnast. Come on you know her. When she gets on the pommel horse it is quite a show

(Catching self.) Or so I've heard

RJ. *(Pulling his leg.)* "So you've heard"

STAN. (Balance beam)

LARRY. What'd you just say?

STAN. It's the

Balance beam

LARRY. *(Psh.)* Okay, sure Stan

  (To the others.) Gym expert over here

VICTOR. Lisa Goldwater, I buy it. What do you think Derek

DEREK. I think,

  I think, that Lisa girl's got...

  (With a crude gesture.) A bright future!

    (Laughter.)

LARRY. *(To* **VICTOR.***)* Maybe Mikey will have some luck with her

VICTOR. *(Ugh.)* I'm worried about that kid. Lately he's been spending all his time on his laptop. Whenever I get home he's all hunched up

RJ & STAN. Porn

VICTOR. No that's not/

RJ & STAN. Porn

VICTOR. No it's those – War of the Worlds? World of War? Hours and hours, playing games with strangers. It's bad enough the twins are doing "concert band" instead of hockey

STAN. *(Bleh.)* Same with Jacob

LARRY. Is he still gonna do baseball?

VICTOR. Oh he sure as hell is still doing baseball

LARRY. So then Coach Larry's got your back

DEREK. Unless he makes Varsity...

VICTOR. Yeah I didn't exactly pass on the Varsity genes

STAN. *(To* **RJ.***)* Victor was a champ back in the day

VICTOR. "Back in the day?"

STAN. *(A joke.)* Well when's the last time you hit a homer?

VICTOR. *(A joke.)* I don't know, when's the last time you fucked Sue?

    (Laughter.)

STAN. *(Not a joke.)* Don't

VICTOR. Loosen up Stan

LARRY. Yeah don't freak on us

STAN. *(Icy.)* I'm not freaking

VICTOR. *(Psh.)* If you say so.

    (Back on this:)

Larry, you should buy her a present

LARRY. What

VICTOR. Leslie. Buy her a present. Just to cover all your bases. Vicky's been getting all pissy about me "working late" these past few weeks so, Bam: I bought her this mini tripod

DEREK. No no he said he "touched her elbow"

LARRY. Her knee actually

DEREK. *(?)* Her knee

LARRY. Boys, when your wife thinks you're cheating on her she doesn't hate *you*. She hates herself. Her desperation level is like a, thirteen out of ten. She wants you to want her. So you touch her knee. You tell her she's pretty. You "see her."

STAN. You, see her?

LARRY. "I just want to feel seen." Leslie says that all the time, when she's sad. It's an easy fix, trust me.

VICTOR. But you still had to fire Maria

LARRY. Oh yeah. Female jealousy, you guys. It's brutal

DEREK. I thought you said you handled it

LARRY. I did handle it

VICTOR. Doesn't really sound like you handled it...

LARRY. There will be other Paolas.

RJ. *(Awkward interruption.)* I don't mess around with immigrant pussy

LARRY. *(Uncomfortable.)* Uh...

RJ. Just seems grimy

DEREK. Huh.

RJ. Not my style

LARRY. *(...)* She's from Brazil

RJ. So?

LARRY. Not, like,

RJ. Whatever, man

LARRY. She's not a

terrorist

RJ. You never know

VICTOR. He's kind of got a point

LARRY. But Brazil. Hello? Brazil! It's. Fancy. Luxurious

DEREK. Carnival

LARRY. Carnival, right

VICTOR. Isn't that what they call waxes? When they take it all off isn't / that

DEREK. A Brazilian, yeah

RJ. What?

STAN. Can someone tell Sue about that?

VICTOR. Vicky was frying eggs the other morning, and something about the way the sun hit her face through the blinds it was just: Hello, Mustache

(Some ad-libs of agreement from the men.)

DEREK. Denise doesn't have that problem

RJ. *(Still on this topic.)* I'm just saying, I like to keep it local. America the beautiful

You should watch it, Larry. Better safe than, *(A crude gesture.)*

LARRY. Sure

...

DEREK. What's your line of work again, "RJ?"

RJ. Tiles

DEREK. Ah

LARRY. *(Bit of a dig.)* So you're a uh, Tiler?

RJ. Yes sir

DEREK. *(Another dig.)* You ever have time to hit the green, when you're not, you know, "tiling"

RJ. You talking like, smoking up?

VICTOR. Ha! Smoking up

STAN. Golf, he's talking golf

RJ. Oh that kind of green

DEREK. Yes indeed

RJ. Can't say I do, no.

LARRY. How's my wife know your wife again? Don't think she ever said

RJ. I dunno, some Women's Club?

VICTOR. *(To **STAN**.)* You hear about that "Women's March" tomorrow?

STAN. Bunch of sore losers

> *(**DEREK** and **LARRY** are still focused on **RJ**.)*

LARRY. *(A judgment.)* So Stockertown, right?

RJ. Yup.

DEREK. *(A judgment.)* How's that

> going

RJ. Used to be pretty good. But these days, *(Disapproving sound.)*

VICTOR. Times have changed

RJ. Times have been fucking bulldozed

VICTOR. I used to recognize every single person in this town. I used to walk through these streets and wave at everyone I passed

DEREK. *(Skeptical...)* Did you though...

VICTOR. Yes Derek, I did.

> But now wherever you turn it's like, who are you? What are you? Are you a, robot? Are you a, Mexican? Are you a –

> *(**LARRY** notices something on the TV.)*

LARRY. Hey, hey, it's happening. It's happening!

STAN. Oh shit

VICTOR. Here we go

RJ. This the oath?

DEREK. Why else would his hand be on the Bible?

VICTOR. Here we go, here we go!

LARRY. *(!)* Andddd

>   *(It happens.)*

>   *(The men erupt into hoots. They are pumped.)*

DEREK. Cheers to a brighter future, boys

>   *(The men all take a glug of their Scotch.)*

>   *(Except* **RJ** *reaches for a beer. And opens it with his teeth.)*

>   *(The men notice.)*

Did you just / *(?)*

LARRY. With your / *(?)*

RJ. That's what back molars are for.

STAN. *(?)* ...Doesn't that chip them / or

RJ. What did you recently get a cleaning or something?

STAN. *(Tight.)* Just asking a question, buddy

>   *(The men consider* **RJ.***)*

RJ. What are you all looking at? It's not a science experiment, you just stick it in there and do the thing.

>   *(The men keep staring at* **RJ.***)*

>   *(A couple of them shake their heads.)*

Unless. You think you can't.

VICTOR. What is that a challenge

RJ. I dunno, is it?

>   *(Oh it is.)*

VICTOR. Gimme one

DEREK. Seriously Victor?

(**RJ** *passes* **VICTOR** *a beer.*)

VICTOR. Alright, one, two, three

    (**VICTOR** *opens a beer with his teeth.*)

RJ. And that's how it's done!

VICTOR. That's how it's motherfucking done

    Your turn Derek

DEREK. What do you mean "my turn"

VICTOR. *(To the other guys.)* He can't do it

DEREK. *(Psh.)* Of course I can do it

VICTOR. *(To the other guys.)* He's worried he'll mess up his teeth, watch, he's –

    (*But then* **DEREK** *grabs a beer.*)

    (*And sticks it in his mouth. And opens it with his teeth.*)

DEREK. *(Smug.)* Simple

RJ. BOOM!

    (**RJ** *tries to chest-bump* **DEREK.**)

DEREK. *(Get the fuck away from me.)* Uh I'm good, RJ. I'm good.

VICTOR. It's all you Larry

    (**VICTOR** *passes* **LARRY** *a beer.*)

LARRY. Well what's the technique? Like which teeth do / you –

RJ. You just bite and bend, there's / no [technique.]

LARRY. Not with the front ones though, right? The, / uh

DEREK. Incisors

LARRY. Incisors yeah

VICTOR. He said the back molars

LARRY. Well there you go! Technique!

VICTOR. That's not technique that's location

LARRY. Okay / well

VICTOR. C'mon, just –

> (**LARRY** *opens his beer with his teeth.*)
>
> (*Kind of. He struggles a bit. He's tentative.*)
>
> (*He clearly doesn't want to mess up his teeth.*)
>
> (*But then –.*)

LARRY. *(Beer cap in mouth.)* Oh oh oh wait for it. Wait for it...

> (*Truly thrilled.*)

I got it! I got it!

RJ. *(...)* Yeah we see that

DEREK. Stan, you're up

STAN. Sorry?

DEREK. Your turn my man

> (**STAN** *has been standing off to the side a little.*)
>
> (**STAN** *does not want to open a beer with his teeth.*)

LARRY. Stan? Hello?

STAN. Yeah I'd rather
sit this one out

RJ. No way

STAN. 'cuse me?

RJ. No fuckin way

VICTOR. We all did it Stan

RJ. What are you scared?

STAN. Psh, yeah right

DEREK. Kinda seems like you're scared

LARRY. Dude are you trembling right now?

STAN. No? What?

RJ. *(Haha!)* You look like you're gonna pee yourself

VICTOR. Oh my god he does, he looks like he's gonna piss all over the floor

LARRY. Don't you dare piss all over my floor, man

STAN. You guys are crazy

DEREK. Just do it Stan, what's the problem

VICTOR. Don't be a little bitch about it!

RJ. Don't be a pussy

STAN. What'd you just say

RJ. I said don't be a –

> (**STAN** *tries to open the beer with his teeth.*)
>
> (*He does a very, very bad job.*)
>
> (*He cuts his lip, hurts himself.*)
>
> (*The bottle cap barely moves.*)
>
> (*The men laugh.*)
>
> (*The men laugh and laugh and laugh.*)

(They are grotesque in their laughter.)

*(**STAN** keeps trying.)*

(He's almost got it.)

(And then:)

STAN. I fucked her.

Lisa Goldwater, the gymnast

ARE YOU LISTENING TO ME I fucked her. Lisa Goldwater

When Sue was at her sister's. Because Sue's always at her sister's. And Jacob was at Brendan's house or Brandon's house I don't –

I saw her waiting outside the gym, shivering. She needed a ride. And she also needed dinner, okay? So I fed her dinner.

And while we sat there, eating, she was all teeth. She was smiling so big, time of her life, it was like we were, we were doing a comedy routine, cracking up, building off each other, and

She was leaning, you know what I mean? You know exactly what I mean. She kept leaning, leaning and I'm not an idiot.

Look, we are living in a shell. This town is a Shell. This town is a shell of a shell of a shell. I have So Fucking Little of what I expected to have

of what I DESERVE to have

And then finally! I can actually GET something! That I want!

And so I did.

Like you wouldn't? I did.

When we're finished she reaches for her headband, it had fallen off – this stupid headband that's like, cheetah print with rainbows, it's, tacky it's, whatever. I'm about to tell her how stupid it is, but I don't.

Because she's lying there with this expression that stops me in my fucking tracks. She's lying there and she's looking at me

with gratitude

I swear to you

with gratitude.

LARRY. Your lip

STAN. What

LARRY. Your lip's bleeding

> (**STAN** *touches his lip.*)
>
> (*It's bleeding.*)

STAN. Well can someone get me a –

> (**LARRY** *passes him a napkin.*)
>
> (**STAN** *presses it against his lip. It's bleeding kind of hard.*)
>
> (*No one says anything for a little while.*)
>
> (*Then.*)
>
> (**RJ** *begins to clap. It's a slow clap.*)
>
> (**RJ** *claps. Claps. Claps.*)
>
> (*Then.*)
>
> (**VICTOR** *joins in.*)

(The clap builds.)

(Clap clap clap clap clap.)

*(**LARRY** and **DEREK** just stand there.)*

RJ. Stan, I did not think you had it in you

VICTOR. Ditto my friend, ditto

RJ. I am deeply sorry for doubting your skills

VICTOR. Guilty as well

(They laugh.)

*(**STAN** doesn't really seem to be paying them much attention. He's in his head, pressing the napkin against his lip.)*

*(**LARRY** looks uncomfortable. **DEREK** looks pissed.)*

DEREK. Are you kidding me right now? We can't be parading this information around

VICTOR. *(Come on.)* We're just having fun

RJ. Larry fucked some immigrant, why the hell are you getting so weird

DEREK. A Brazilian housekeeper is different / than

RJ. Different than a born and bred American woman? I'd say so

DEREK. Woman? She's in high school.

VICTOR. She's a senior

DEREK. So?

VICTOR. So she's eighteen

...Right?

STAN. Nineteen

VICTOR. She's nineteen!

LARRY. *(Starting to feel uncomfortable.)* That's. Yeah. nineteen. That's. Yeah.

DEREK. Doesn't Madison have a birthday coming up, Larry?

LARRY. Uh. Yeah. She's uh, she's turning sixteen.

DEREK. Same with Brianne

RJ. You guys have daughters?

LARRY. Yep

RJ. You better keep 'em in line. With Stan Newkirk roaming free and all

VICTOR. *(Good one!)* Yikes!

DEREK. I would never in a million years leave Brianne out to dry like that

STAN. *(Defensive.)* I didn't fuck a sixteen-year-old

DEREK. Like three years is that different

VICTOR. Hey a lot happens in those three years

STAN. I didn't fuck anyone's daughter!

LARRY. Well she is

Someone's daughter

STAN. Yeah okay she's Someone's Daughter obviously but

I basically watched Brianne grow up, that's disgusting

DEREK. Well I don't know what you're gonna do next!

VICTOR. Come on it's not like he's Diseased

STAN. Yeah! It's not like I'm running around ready to scoop up any girl I see shivering outside the gym

LARRY. Okay, that's

See? That's. Good

RJ. This is hilarious. You are like, dripping in jealousy, Derek. Wipe yourself down, man

>   (**DEREK** *considers* **RJ**. *It's icy.*)

DEREK. Who even invited this guy?

RJ. It really drives you crazy that little Stan / over here

STAN. "Little?"

RJ. snatched up the prize, and you did not.

DEREK. Don't think of teenagers as prizes, but maybe that's common for Your Kind

RJ. The fuck you just say?

LARRY. Hey hey hey hey

RJ. You were just talking about how hot this girl was, earlier today

DEREK. *(Psh.)* I said she had a bright future

RJ. Oh yeah, and we all took that super seriously

DEREK. I didn't say I would Fuck Her

RJ. Cuz thinking someone's sexy never means we want to have sex with them

DEREK. You're walking a thin line, you know that?

RJ. And you sit behind a desk all day, while I'm doing man's work: sanding, troweling, / and pumping grout

DEREK. Is that supposed to intimidate me? I could liquidate your assets

RJ. *(Nerdy voice.)* "I could liquidate your assets"

DEREK. I could Own you

>   (**RJ** *approaches* **DEREK** *aggressively.*)

>   (**LARRY** *steps between them.*)

LARRY. Let's just settle down guys

    (**DEREK** *considers* **STAN.**)

DEREK. Stan, I'm a pillar of this community, okay? I Cannot be implicated

LARRY. *(Getting a little nervous...)* Woah what do you mean, implicated

STAN. *(Pissed.)* No one is implicated in anything! You all have absolutely nothing to do with this. This belongs to me! This is mine.

    (**STAN**'s *lip starts to bleed again.*)

(Stupid lip.) I'm gonna –

    (*He presses his lip with a napkin.*)

    (*And exits for the bathroom.*)

LARRY. Okay. This is Stan's, Thing. He, clarified. So, are we cool?

VICTOR. What are you looking at me for? I'm fine

LARRY. Derek?

DEREK. *What* Larry

LARRY. You're cool. Right?

VICTOR. Or are you gonna be a narc about it?

RJ. *(To himself.)* He would never

DEREK. You want to say that a little louder?

LARRY. Okay let's / –

RJ. You would never.

DEREK. What the / [Fuck.]

RJ. Derek, "a Pillar of this Community." Father of the Year. Man of the Year. What a Good Guy. Such a Good Guy would never stand for this. Would never drool over a young girl and her *(Impersonating* **DEREK,** *with gesture.)* "bright future."

Or would he.

Oh am I wrong? You gonna rat on Stan? You gonna rat on Your Boy? No way. You can get on your fucking high horse all you want but you know, you know you're not going to do anything. Except wag your finger, for a second. And then you'll go "hit the green" or whatever the fuck. Then you'll just sit back and relax, staring at your perfect little lawn and your perfect little life.

Won't you. Won't you?

Scene Three

(Suddenly we're in a different living room.)

(This one is in Brooklyn. Exposed brick. Mason jars. Maybe a few packing boxes.)

(It's cramped and a little sadly decorated, but it's clear that someone's trying.)

*(**STAN**, who is now **SASHA**, bursts back on stage. She's holding a box of donuts.)*

*(**LARRY, DEREK**, and **VICTOR** are now **LUCY, DANA**, and **VIVIAN**. **RJ** is not present.)*

(It is the end of February 2017.)

LUCY. Guys I can't stop reading the news in bed, on my phone.

DANA, VIVIAN & SASHA. Same

LUCY. I wake up, check my email, check *The New York Times*, check my apps, and then I'm horizontal for forty-five minutes in a fetal position of dread

VIVIAN. Oh absolutely same

LUCY. It's like oh great, another terrible executive order, oh great, more travel bans and now a budget for building "the wall." And then, cool, here's a photo of my ex with some woman with perfect bangs wearing a jumpsuit she sewed herself

SASHA. I bought a digital alarm clock

LUCY. I should do that

SASHA. But I still scroll on my phone first thing in the morning. It's just that I'm like, standing upright while I'm doing it

LUCY. Well that's, slightly better

DANA. I thought you said you were starting your days meditating?

LUCY. I've been inconsistent

VIVIAN. Whatever I don't know how we're supposed to be zen right now

DANA. Well yeah I don't think we Are supposed to be zen right now

SASHA. I turned off my Breaking News alerts is that bad?

VIVIAN. I've been watching so much reality TV

LUCY. I've been watching *Handmaid's Tale*

VIVIAN. Oh I can't even touch that

DANA. I've been taking a boxing class

LUCY. How is it?

DANA. I punch a bag for an hour and it feels great?

VIVIAN. Yeah I've been trying to run more for the endorphins

SASHA. I've kind of just been eating my feelings.

Which is why I brought these!

> (**SASHA** *displays her box of donuts, proudly.*)

> (*The others are excited.*)

LUCY. *(!)* Those look incredible

DANA. *(Re: the donuts.)* Lucy do you want to grab some plates?

LUCY. Sure!

Oh wait – I still haven't bought a full set of dishware. I just have, one plate and one bowl. For me

DANA. Oh. Okay.

VIVIAN. Moving is hell

LUCY. Truly

SASHA. The new place is looking great so far though!

DANA. Yeah it's really,

cozy!

LUCY. *(…)* Thanks. You don't think it's. Cramped?

DANA, VIVIAN & SASHA. No no no, not at all, [etc.]

> *(They look around the apartment.)*

> *(It's cramped.)*

LUCY. Well we don't really need plates, right? Are people cool with just using their, hands?

DANA. *(Doesn't love this.)* Yeah, whatever

SASHA. Dibs on this caramel one

> *(They all reach for a donut. But* **VIVIAN** *takes her hand away.)*

VIVIAN. Wait – where did you say these were from, Sasha?

SASHA. Glazed and Amazed

LUCY. My favorite

VIVIAN. Ohhhh. Okay. Then I think I'm gonna pass.

SASHA. There's a gluten-free one for you, Vivian

> *(***SASHA*** *takes a big bite of her donut.)*

VIVIAN. No no it's not that. I'm just

I'm really trying to walk the walk about buying and consuming local. It's, whatever

LUCY. Glazed and Amazed is local

VIVIAN. Not anymore. They've got branches in like, every borough. It's a full-on corporation now.

SASHA. *(Mouth full.)* That sucks...

LUCY. *(Overlapping.)* I didn't know...

DANA. *(Overlapping.)* Yeah I had no idea...

> (**LUCY** *and* **DANA** *put their donuts back in the box.*)

VIVIAN. Oh I SO didn't mean to like, stop you guys from eating them!

Seriously. Eat. Seriously! Eat!

> (**SASHA** *takes her up on that offer. She takes another bite of the donut.*)

> (*The others don't touch theirs.*)

> (*Awkward.*)

DANA. We'll donate them.

VIVIAN. That's a great idea Dana

SASHA. *(...)* But we've already, touched them. Can we / really *(?)*

LUCY. I thought food donations had to be like

canned goods?

DANA. Not necessarily

VIVIAN. I passed a homeless man on my way over here. I'm sure he would love these

SASHA. *(...)* Oh he really would

LUCY. What if he's

diabetic

DANA. Lucy come on. That's kind of a stereotype.

Anyway should we get started?

(**SASHA** *has been trying to secretly keep eating her donut.*)

Secretary Sasha?

SASHA. *(Caught.)* Yes!

(Consulting notes.) Um, okay – according to my notes, tonight's intention is: Determining our spring action item. Does anyone have anything?

DANA. Actually, yeah, I do. I think we should host a fundraiser. At a bar. In the neighborhood.

LUCY. For the ACLU

DANA. Or BLM

LUCY. Or NARAL

SASHA. Or CAIR

VIVIAN. But wait

What bar would we do this at?

LUCY. I'm sure Winterhill would be interested

DANA. *(!)* Winterhill is terrible

VIVIAN. *(!)* That place is like Gentrification 101!

SASHA. *(!)* Their ad campaign?

LUCY. Ohmygod I'm kidding I'm totally kidding

VIVIAN. Okay, I was gonna say...

LUCY. I can't believe you guys thought I was Condoning Gentrification

DANA. Dude. Chill.

SASHA. I'm pretty sure Winterhill's gonna close down. They've been getting terrible Yelp reviews

VIVIAN. Yeah I wrote one.

SASHA. Oh my god go Vivian!!

LUCY. Seriously though, what about Queen Tilda's?

VIVIAN. That place is really cute

DANA. I don't know... Queen Tilda's is like a block away from Winterhill

LUCY. Yeah but it's not associated / with

DANA. Right / but

LUCY. It's run by someone who's lived here for a really long time

DANA. Is it?

LUCY. Pedro!

SASHA. Oh yeah Pedro!

LUCY. Pedro is super nice

VIVIAN. Their cocktails Are pricey though...

LUCY. But they have a happy hour. And three dollar tamales

SASHA. I do love those tamales...

DANA. I just want to be clear like, I know by hosting this bar night we are definitely excluding people who can't afford the price of a drink and I just want to be upfront like I recognize that.

VIVIAN. Thank you.

DANA. You're welcome.

LUCY. *(New idea.)* What about a march?

DANA. *(Um?)* Aren't we still discussing the bar night?

LUCY. Oh I thought we were doing popcorn style?

SASHA. *(Looking over notes.)* Last meeting we did decide on popcorn style as a brainstorming strategy

DANA. Okay well, didn't a march kind of, already happen

LUCY. What do you mean?

DANA. *(Duh.)* The Women's March

LUCY. *(?)* That was in January

VIVIAN. I'm Still impressed with all the signs we made

DANA. I mean yeah they were epic

SASHA. Guys I've been working on a little collage, of photos from the march

VIVIAN. Oh that's so cute

Can we vet them first?

LUCY. Definitely put in that group shot. The one where we're angry

VIVIAN. Oh yeah the one with the fists, use that one

SASHA. It just sucks KJ isn't in any of the photos

VIVIAN. I can't believe she didn't come.

Dana didn't you text her?

DANA. Yeah of course

LUCY. The thing is, we shouldn't just stop at One march. We need to keep up the momentum

SASHA. That's so true actually

DANA. Well if we did another one, what would it be for?

LUCY. *(Considers...)* How about a march for...

VIVIAN. Intersectionality!

LUCY. Oh that's good

SASHA. That's really good

DANA. Is it though...

VIVIAN. Do you not want to honor intersectionality?

DANA. What? No I totally want to honor intersectionality

VIVIAN. Awesome

DANA. I am hyper-devoted to intersectionality, obviously. But. That doesn't mean it's the best theme for a march

VIVIAN. *(Slightly defensive.)* Okay. I was just brainstorming, popcorn style.

> *(VIVIAN's phone buzzes.)*

> *(She looks at it. Scrolls.)*

SASHA. Isn't it wild that the next generation will literally come out of the womb already knowing what intersectionality is?

LUCY. Well not, literally

SASHA. Yeah yeah, but the next generation will be ten steps ahead of us. Like our kids will instantly know All the terminology

DANA. Not everyone wants kids

SASHA. I mean IF we have kids, sorry, If we have kids /

VIVIAN. *(Re: phone.)* Wait guys, there's a march happening in the park! I just found it on Facebook! Maybe we could team up with them. It's for

> *(Looking at phone.)*

Another police shooting

DANA. Fuck.

LUCY. Fuck.

SASHA. Fuck.

VIVIAN. We should go.

DANA. We should definitely go.

LUCY. When is it?

VIVIAN. It's!

Oh it's...

Tomorrow

> *(The group deflates.)*

> *(To* **LUCY**.*)* Kim's bridal shower is tomorrow

LUCY. I know...

VIVIAN. I think it would be pretty bad if / we

LUCY. If we bailed, yeah.

DANA. If I ever get married, I am saying No Thank You to a bridal shower. And, *I'm* going to propose

SASHA. *(?!)* You're gonna propose to Mike

DANA. Not like, Tomorrow but, in a couple years, if we're still together, then,

Yeah. Why wait for some "tradition" if you know what you want?

VIVIAN. That is Fierce

SASHA. That's amazing

DANA. It shouldn't be amazing

LUCY. *(Let's stop...)* Can you go to the march tomorrow, Dana?

DANA. Sadly I can't. I got tickets to see that new documentary about immigration detention centers

SASHA. I've been meaning to see that

DANA. Yeah I can't wait

VIVIAN. The trailer was SO sad

LUCY. *(Competitive.)* It's life-changing. I was ugly-crying during the whole thing.

DANA. *(...)* Oh. You've

already seen it?

LUCY. Yeah, opening night.

DANA. *(...)* Wow, commitment

LUCY. *(A dig.)* It's just a really important story so, I didn't want to waste time.

DANA. Sure sure

Why can't you march, Sasha?

SASHA. I'm um

I'm

Going on a date

VIVIAN. Don't tell me it's with Nick

DANA. Do not say Nick

SASHA. It's

LUCY. Oh god

SASHA. ...Nick

DANA. Sasha!

VIVIAN. Sasha what the fuck! We talked about this

SASHA. I KNOW he works for a hedge fund but he has a lot of student loans to pay off!

DANA. *(Has never had any student loans.)* There are Always other ways

LUCY. *(Still dealing with student loans.)* Well student loans Do suck...

SASHA. *(Definitely still dealing with student loans.)* (yeah they really really suck)

VIVIAN. *(Has also never had any student loans.)* No one's saying they don't suck! But you have to decide what kind of person you are, you know? Everyone decides how they want to live their values.

Sasha, judgment-free zone but, as your Accountability Partner I'm not thrilled about this

SASHA. I know, I know

LUCY. *(Trying...)* Well what are you and Nick gonna do?

SASHA. We're um

seeing a movie

LUCY. The immigration documentary?

SASHA. Um no. Not the

Not that

VIVIAN. Okay

SASHA. Yeah.

DANA. ...So what are you seeing

SASHA. *(Can barely say it.)* The

...

new

movie

LUCY. The /

SASHA. *(Shame shame shame.)* with Emma Stone

(A collective groan.)

DANA. You are NOT seeing that movie

VIVIAN. I'm boycotting that movie. Have you seen the trailer? / It's

LUCY. Soooo many white people

SASHA. *(Ashamed.)* You're right you're right

VIVIAN. Isn't that a podcast? Sooo Many White People?

DANA. Wait does this mean we're all busy tomorrow?

LUCY. Well. If we do our own, we'll just make sure it's on a night that everyone's free.

I'm happy to spearhead

SASHA. A march does sound kind of fun...

>   (**DANA** *shoots* **SASHA** *a look.*)

(Haha...) But so does a bar night

DANA. Let's add a vote to the top of the next meeting.

SASHA. Done.

All in favor of moving on?

LUCY.	**VIVIAN.**	**DANA.**
Sure	Yes please	Fine

SASHA. *(Consulting agenda.)* Because it's tiiiime for...

(Jokey.) the renowned, the illustrious, the grandest, the greatest...

The Bad Ass Woman Awards!

>   (**SASHA, LUCY, DANA,** *and* **VIVIAN** *cheer!!*)

Alright I've got one. My personal award for Bad Ass Woman of the week goes to...

Vivian!

VIVIAN. Awww no way

>   (**SASHA** *bestows the Bad Ass Woman award onto* **VIVIAN.***)*
>
>   *(The Bad Ass Woman award is a necklace made out of tampons.)*
>
>   (**VIVIAN** *is thrilled.*)
>
>   (**SASHA** *clears her throat and reads from a piece of paper.*)

SASHA. This week, Vivian channeled her divine feminine genius and flicked two middle fingers at the patriarchy. Because this week, Vivian, our very own Vivian, had the persistence, strength, and courage to...

Successfully negotiate a raise with her *male* boss!

DANA. You stood up to Watkins?

VIVIAN. *(Proud.)* I stood up to Watkins

LUCY. That's super bad ass Vivian

VIVIAN. Sasha, didn't you have a meeting with your boss recently? About a possible raise?

DANA. Oh yeah how did that go?

SASHA. Um well...

He was just meeting with me to go over some spreadsheets and I thought I would try to like, Shoehorn the raise conversation in

VIVIAN. No no no you need to call a separate meeting

LUCY. You need to be the assertive one

VIVIAN. If you don't start being assertive, you're going to be treated inferior

DANA. *(Correction:)* Wait so you're saying she needs to

Lean in?

VIVIAN. Haha! I mean that book is problematic

DANA. That book is very problematic

VIVIAN. But also like...

Also like in a way, yeah. Lean In

SASHA. I just don't even know that works

VIVIAN. *(This is how it works:)* Some dude puts his feet on the desk and says, "yo I want to be paid more"

SASHA. *(...)* Did you put your

feet on the desk, Vivian?

VIVIAN. No Sasha, I did not put my feet on the desk. But at a certain point I did have to say: Fuck it. I deserve this. WE deserve this

LUCY. Hell yeah

DANA. She's not wrong

VIVIAN. You've really got to own your power, Sasha. *(Cheery.)* No matter who you have to step on along the way.

DANA. Anyone else? Anyone have awards to give out?

VIVIAN. Oh! I do

My personal award for Bad Ass Woman of the week goes to someone who has steadily been pushing back against male conceptions of female beauty. And that is...

Lucy!

> (DANA *and* SASHA *cheer!*)

> (DANA *is probably slightly amused by this.*)

> (VIVIAN *bestows another tampon necklace onto* LUCY.)

LUCY. Wait what

VIVIAN. I've just noticed that you haven't been shaving your legs. And I think that's really cool. That's like, really bad ass

SASHA. Yeah! Fuck shaving!

LUCY. Oh haha thanks!

DANA. *(...)* What's wrong

LUCY. Nothing

VIVIAN. You're being. Weird

LUCY. It's just that

Well it's winter.

VIVIAN. *(?)* Okay

LUCY. Do you all shave your legs during the

winter?

> *(Yes. They do.)*

VIVIAN. I've been getting waxed, actually

LUCY. You wax your legs?

VIVIAN. Yeah your hair grows back so much slower

LUCY. Doesn't that get

expensive

VIVIAN. It's worth it.

SASHA. *(...)* Maybe I should make a waxing appointment

DANA. Only if you want to, Sasha! None of us should feel
Obligated to do any of this

VIVIAN. That's why I thought what Lucy was doing was so
bad ass

LUCY. Thanks

VIVIAN. Well – Hang on. So you're saying this was like

Unintentional?

LUCY. I mean, kind of? I mean. Yeah

VIVIAN, SASHA & DANA. Ohhhhh, okay [etc.]

VIVIAN. Well. Maybe next week

> *(**VIVIAN** takes the tampon necklace off **LUCY**.)*

LUCY. What?

(**LUCY** *looks kind of crushed. She stands apart from the other women.*)

SASHA. Wait so what's the name of your waxing place?

VIVIAN. Wax on Fifth. They do legs, Brazilians, everything

DANA. Is it Fifth in Brooklyn or Fifth in Manhattan

VIVIAN. It's Fifth in /

LUCY. Oh! You guys! I have something I wanted to share. With the group. As long as no one has any more awards to give out?

(*Quick scan. No one has any more awards.*)

Ok so. I read this article the other day about this really cool thing that a lot of social justice groups are doing. It's called a

Well it has kind of a weird name but it's called a

(white guilt) ritual

SASHA. A

what?

LUCY. Um. A

White Guilt Ritual

DANA. (...) Ritual?

VIVIAN. How does it work?

LUCY. Well first we need a mirror. And (*Indicates her mirror.*) I have a mirror.

SASHA. Yeah great touch by the way

(*The women approach the mirror.*)

(*We don't see it, but they do. The mirror is where the audience sits.*)

LUCY. So the article says: we stand here. And stare at our reflections. And

(She looks at her phone.)

"Encounter our flaws, mistakes, and, most importantly, prejudices."

DANA. *(?)* Just by, staring

LUCY. We'll we're supposed to generate like a, catalogue of wrongdoing

And then we do a purging

VIVIAN. Okay.

Wait how do we do a purging?

*(**LUCY** takes out her phone again.)*

LUCY. *(Skimming article.)* They say we should do a mantra. To purge our sins

DANA. Did you find this on like a, religious website?

LUCY. *(!)* What? No

DANA. *(...)* The word "sin"? That's like, pro-life language

LUCY. This is definitely not connected to pro-life, I promise

VIVIAN. Let's just let her do her thing, Dana

DANA. Fine, fine. Whatever.

LUCY. Okay. Is everybody ready?

Anddddd

Go

(They stare at themselves in the mirror.)

(They stare.)

SASHA. Are we supposed to /

VIVIAN. Sasha, come on

SASHA. I'm just wondering: are we supposed to. Say it out loud? The things we feel guilty for? Or are we supposed to just say it in our heads

to ourselves

(Everyone looks at LUCY.*)*

LUCY. Um well. As the leader of this exercise I think,

We can just say it in our heads

DANA, VIVIAN & SASHA. *(Relieved.)* Okay cool; Great; Sounds good [etc.]

(They stare.)

(They stare.)

SASHA. Are you guys working chronologically / or

VIVIAN. *(Annoyed.)* What, Sasha?

SASHA. I was just wondering how people are like, cataloguing their white guilt memories

VIVIAN. I don't think we're supposed to take breaks like this

LUCY. Yeah we're definitely not

(The women stare.)

(The women stare.)

(The women stare.)

(Out of the blue:)

I'm sorry. I'm sorry /

DANA. What are you doing?

LUCY. Oh this is the mantra. For the purging

VIVIAN. I'm sorry / I'm sorry

LUCY. Perfect

LUCY, VIVIAN, SASHA & DANA. I'm sorry I'm sorry I'm sorry
I'm sorry I'm sorry I'm sorry

> *(The women keep saying they're sorry.)*
>
> *(Four white women stare at themselves in the mirror, apologizing.)*
>
> *(This reaches a kind of crescendo.)*
>
> *(At a certain point:)*

LUCY. Wow

VIVIAN. Woah

SASHA. Woooow

LUCY. I feel

Lighter!

SASHA & VIVIAN. Me too I totally feel lighter!; Yeah yes
lighter; Uh huh same [etc.]

LUCY. Not that this is The Answer, obviously

DANA. Obviously

LUCY. But. This is a start.

(...is it?)

VIVIAN. I feel like we should take a picture. To document
this.

LUCY. Great call

> *(**VIVIAN** takes out her phone to take a selfie.)*

VIVIAN. "Bad Ass Women Make Better Allies" on three!

One, two, three –

*(The group repeats, "Bad Ass Women Make
Better Allies" while they pose for a mirror
selfie.)*

VIVIAN. *(While posting.)* I'm tagging all of you

(Brief brief beat.)

Should I also tag

KJ

SASHA. I wish she were here

LUCY. I love KJ

VIVIAN. Same

SASHA. Same

VIVIAN. Have you heard from her lately, Dana?

DANA. Sure we text all the time

VIVIAN. But, have you heard from her about why she hasn't been here?

SASHA. I thought you said she had a really good time at the meetings she came to

DANA. Yeah yeah she did

VIVIAN. *(An idea.)* You know the 2 train's been down for awhile

DANA. *(No big deal.)* And also nights can be hard for people

SASHA. I Have seen KJ post stories where she's snuggling with her laptop in bed after an intense day of work

LUCY. Maybe we should try meeting on weekends

VIVIAN. Like brunch themed!

SASHA. I could bring donuts again!

Or maybe

bagels

VIVIAN. Wait Sasha, you didn't forget to invite her to the meeting, did you?

SASHA. It wasn't my turn to email

It was Lucy's

(They all look at **LUCY.***)*

LUCY. No of course I didn't forget!

DANA. Are you sure?

VIVIAN. It would explain a lot if you did

*(***LUCY** *takes out her phone to check.)*

LUCY. No it's right here. I invited her.

But

(Shit)

DANA. What?

LUCY. I Did forget to email her the agenda

SASHA. Some people really need agendas...

VIVIAN. What if she was waiting for it All night, but it never came

LUCY. Or maybe she's not here for some other reason guys, come on

SASHA. Oh my god. What if one of us did something

Bad

DANA. Woah, what?

VIVIAN. I'm like seriously racking my brain trying to remember the last meeting she was at

SASHA. We started with those journaling prompts, and then we went around and shared our reflections

VIVIAN. Ohh right

LUCY. You Were kind of taking up a lot of space during the sharing portion, Vivian – when you told that story about the woman who used to be your nanny

VIVIAN. *(…)* I didn't think that story was that long

LUCY. It was

VIVIAN. Well in the spirit of calling you in, Lucy: what You shared that night might have made KJ feel uncomfortable

LUCY. Why?

VIVIAN. You kept talking about how you're really invested in non-monogamy now and how radical that is and it's like, there are other priorities

LUCY. I didn't say that was the Only thing I'm invested in

Oh my god does she think it's the only thing I'm invested in?

DANA. *(Kind of a joke.)* It's possible

LUCY. Dana just as a reminder, sometimes you forget to use I statements

DANA. *(?)* Thanks for the heads up

(**SASHA, VIVIAN,** *and* **LUCY** *start to spiral.*)

SASHA. Did I interrupt her while she was speaking?

VIVIAN. Maybe I didn't say thank you when she held the door for me

LUCY. Yeah I think I remember that

VIVIAN. Wait really?

DANA. Guys, calm down

LUCY. Maybe I should have asked her to be my partner when we got into breakout groups

SASHA. Maybe I should have given her a Bad Ass Woman award

VIVIAN. Oh my god does KJ hate us??

DANA. What are you talking about?

LUCY. She totally hates us

SASHA. I won't be able to handle it if she does

VIVIAN. Yeah I'm kind of freaking out

DANA. Okay you all need to chill

VIVIAN. But I'm like Really freaking out

LUCY. Yeah I don't love this feeling

SASHA. Me neither

VIVIAN. I'm like REALLY FREAKING OUT!

Scene Four

(Instantly:)

(The first week of March 2017.)

*(**KJ** enters. She's telling a story.)*

*(Everyone except **DANA** vanishes.)*

KJ. So – okay so,

Trevor has an elaborate morning, ritual. Skincare is, important to him. Cystic acne when he was in 8th grade or something? Everyone made fun of him? I don't know. It was very formative to his, whatever. So he spends a long time in there. Like a loooong time. Every morning

DANA. You mean in the bathroom

KJ. Yes. And he locks the door. When he's in there, doing his face stuff, the bathroom becomes, His Space. And I better not disrupt it

DANA. That sounds /

KJ. Yeah it's a lot.

And this morning, okay so this morning, he's in there and the door's locked, of course, but the problem is

The problem is I have to go to the bathroom. Like I Really have to go to the bathroom

DANA. Oh no

KJ. So I knock. And he's all, "just a minute" through the door but he kind of barks it, like I can Hear the deep irritation bordering on resentment in his voice. He doesn't say it but I know, I Know he's thinking: we went over this, you don't disturb me right now

DANA. Trevor, come on

KJ. So he's not going to budge. And he'll be in there for at least another twenty, fifteen minimum. But I'm about to –

I mean it feels like I'm about to piss my pants

DANA. Ohhh no

KJ. And what am I supposed to do? Find that neighbor I sometimes say hi to on the stairs? Plus I don't have time to walk down to the street, and the hostess at that new bougie breakfast place wouldn't have let me in anyway so I

Ok I'm not proud of this but I

I rolled down my pants

And I

I peed in our garbage can

DANA. No

KJ. Yes

DANA. No!

KJ. There was no other option! And then I tied the bag up nice and tight and took it to the bins on the curb

DANA. When did he come out of the bathroom??

KJ. A full twenty-five minutes later

DANA. Twenty-five!

KJ. Without even the tiniest sliver of an idea of what just went down

DANA. Oh my god

And then you just said like, I made coffee??

KJ. No I said I want to break up.

DANA. Oh!

KJ. If I am peeing in a trash can in our apartment it's time to end things.

So yeah. That was my morning.

DANA. Woah. Are you okay?

KJ. Is it bad to say...yes?

DANA. Not at all

KJ. I feel like there's a lightness. A weight has been –

No, not "a weight has been lifted," that's such a cliché. But something, snapped. I don't know. It feels nice.

DANA. That's great!

KJ. But I Was late to work because we had to, sort everything out

DANA. *(Damn.)* Right

KJ. Which sucked because my caseload has been Insane lately. And the Harvard grandpas keep sizing me up

DANA. Still?

KJ. For sure still. And they insist on calling me Keisha

DANA. Shit really

KJ. Even though I'm like dude, I go by KJ, at the top of all my briefs it's KJ

DANA. Fucking old white men

KJ. Fucking old white men!

> *(Maybe it's now we see that they're at a bar.)*

> *(They sip drinks. They pick at a basket of fries.)*

DANA. I like this place

KJ. It's cute, right?

DANA. It kind of reminds me of that bar we used to go to on Damen. What was it called

KJ. *(Really?)* The Faucet

DANA. No no no

KJ. *(Weird memories.)* Can't believe how much time I spent there

DANA. *(Didn't really hear her.)* No I'm talking about that place we would go when we were trying to be fancy

KJ. The Violet Room

DANA. Slightly less fancy

KJ. Oh That Place, what was it called, started with an N maybe?

KJ & DANA. *(Recognition.)* Nico's!

KJ. God remember how old we seemed to ourselves?

DANA. Oh yeah we thought we were Ancient

KJ. Senior year, "going into the city"

DANA. But we were babies

KJ. We were children.

And remember Mike back then?

DANA. I do not miss that version of him

(Some laughter.)

KJ. He grew into himself didn't he

DANA. Or just,

grew out of all that bro energy

KJ. How are you guys though?

DANA. He's good, we're good

(Realizing.)

DANA. I mean, other than the world imploding. Obviously

KJ. Right.

DANA. *(Noticing.)* Do they ever do shows? On that stage over there?

KJ. On the weekends, yeah.

I've performed here a couple of times with my band

DANA. *(?!?)* You're in a band? Since when??

KJ. Since last fall

Haven't we talked about this?

DANA. I think you're thinking of someone else

KJ. No I'm pretty sure we've talked about this

DANA. So I know you're balancing your crazy caseload – and your band – but, is there any chance you're free next Thursday night or is that just like a non-starter with your schedule?

KJ. *(Jogging brain.)* Um, next Thursday next Thursday

Why

DANA. I'm hosting this bar night fundraiser, with my group. You know my post-election, social justice working group. We need to think of an actual name one of these days / but

KJ. Ohhh right right. Your group

DANA. But it's in Crown Heights. So the commute for you might suck

KJ. Yeah it's kind of a slog

DANA. Total slog.

We should host events around here

KJ. It's fine, it's fine

DANA. No seriously. Or I was even thinking, the group could have meetings at your place sometimes.

If it would be easier for you to attend, I mean. Since I know your schedule is so hectic

KJ. Oh –

DANA. And I could help out of course with like set up and food and stuff

KJ. Yeah I don't know...

Do you really think the other girls would want to take the train All the Way Up Here

DANA. For you? Absolutely. We miss you!

KJ. What do you guys miss about me

DANA. *(A joke.)* Oh fishing for compliments? Very subtle

KJ. No really. What do you guys miss about me

DANA. Well. For one,

your lawyer expertise in the room

KJ. I do copyright law

DANA. No I know, I know

KJ. So that's very different than like, civil rights litigation

DANA. Yeah, yes, of course

KJ. I didn't say much at the meetings you brought me to

DANA. But you were listening

KJ. Sometimes I was spacing out

DANA. That's

fine

KJ. You guys didn't really talk about

Anything

DANA. Fair.

That's why I'm so excited about this bar night. We're raising money for –

Well we haven't decided yet but I want to pull for Brooklyn Community Bail Fund

…

Oh is that not a good idea

KJ. Why wouldn't it be

DANA. You just didn't react so I – nevermind

I want there to be a phone bank in the back, too, for people to call their representatives

KJ. *(?)* Isn't it a Bar

Night

DANA. *(…)* People can

leave messages.

Anyway it would be great if you could be there

KJ. Yeah – it just

It might be tough

DANA. Makes sense

KJ. *(…)* With my schedule

DANA. Your schedule, yes.

Plus

(Gossip mode.)

I know those girls can be a lot

KJ. *(Weakly trying.)* No they're cool

(Do they both laugh a little?)

DANA. It's okay I know, I know

Like Sasha? She's so clueless. She's been seeing this finance guy, some "fiscal conservative" or whatever

KJ. Yeah that's not actually a thing

DANA. Exactly! And I think his shitty politics might be rubbing off on her – we're trying to intervene.

Or Vivian – she can't stop flaunting how she's "buying and consuming local"

KJ. Classic

DANA. So irritating. And she's been pulling this boss lady feminism shit all the time lately

KJ. Also classic

DANA. Yes! And Lucy can be Super problematic. And kind of reckless. She's dating like four different people right now I don't even [know.]

I get it. I know they can be annoying. And absurd.

KJ. Yeah.

DANA. *(...)* Right.

Did they ever make you feel uncomfortable? At the meetings you went to?

KJ. What do you mean uncomfortable

DANA. Whatever that means to you. I just –

I really want to give you the space to let me know if anything happened. Like if anyone said something, or

Did they say something to you?

KJ. Say something? I don't / *(?)*

DANA. Did they say something, insensitive or – something that offended you, or –?

I know this is my job, like to – you can tell me.

KJ. Um. No.

No one said anything like that.

DANA. Okay that's great. That is – such a relief. They've all been acting really weird about why you haven't been back and I was like guys, chill, but I just wanted to check /

KJ. Wait is this why you texted me to hang? To get me to come back to your group?

DANA. No! I mean it's something I wanted to discuss but it's not the / only

KJ. Okay I was gonna say...

Because if you were like, "We're trying to be more aware of our blind spots and invite New Perspectives," or /

DANA. *(Playing along.)* "This is such an important moment and we Really need your voice"

KJ. "We're trying to Unlearn"

DANA. "We trying to Do the Work"

KJ. Oh definitely do the work. "We want to be Better Allies."

DANA. "We want to hear what You have to tell us because we are Finally Paying Attention"

KJ. "Now more than / ever"

DANA. Now more than ever! Right

KJ. And then we'd have to take a photo

DANA. And post it

KJ. And the caption would be a row of those little fist emojis in all different skin tones, and it would get like, one hundred likes

DANA. *(Serious.)* Oh over one hundred, easily

(Their laughter peters out.)

(They consider each other.)

White people are so stupid.

...

KJ. Dana you know that you're

also white

right

DANA. *(?)* Uh, I do, yes. I'm aware

KJ. Because sometimes you

[   ]

DANA. What

KJ. Nothing. Nevermind

How's your drink?

*(**DANA** sips.)*

DANA. Kind of amazing.

KJ. Do you remember when we would get that Dole fruit juice out of the dorm vending machines, and mix it with *(Can't remember.)* /

DANA. *(Ugh.)* Burnett's

KJ. *(Ugh.)* Burnett's!

DANA. Truly

vile

KJ. Yeah Why did we do that to ourselves?

DANA. I think it had a pretty bottle

KJ. I think it was cheap

(They smile and laugh with each other.)

(Then.)

DANA. I'm really glad we did this

KJ. Me too

DANA. *(Jokey.)* You're like the busiest person I know

KJ. Yeah I need to tone it down

DANA. *(Jokey.)* Sometimes when I text you I'm like, will I hear from her in two hours? Two days?

Two weeks

KJ. I knowww. I wish there were a "mark unread" feature for texts

DANA. *(Jokey.)* They really should get on that shouldn't they

KJ. Seriously

DANA. *(Not so jokey…)* Yeah

[   ]

I don't want to make this like a whole Thing but

Sometimes

it feels like you're ignoring me?

KJ. What? I just have a lot on my plate

DANA. Totally. I get it.

It's just like –

It happens a lot?

Like in January

KJ. January? Are we really / *(?)*

DANA. I mean the Women's March. The morning of the Women's March I thought we were, going to go

together

Did you even go?

KJ. No. No I didn't

DANA. Oh. Okay

Why

KJ. Because I didn't want to

DANA. Okay

But I thought we were on the same page about –

It was a really powerful day I figured you would want to be there

KJ. Yeah, I didn't. It wasn't for me.

DANA. What? Of course it was. Of course it [   ] It –

Was it? Was – Unless [   ]

I'm being really awkward

> (**DANA** *stuffs herself with French fries throughout the following.*)

Like I'm very familiar with the history of – like white women have been The Worst for So Long and that Includes Today – I own that, I totally own that. But also I'm [   ]

Like I've seen those women – the women you're – and, I'm not

like them

right?

KJ. Who is "them"

DANA. I'm different

Right? Than the other [   ]

DANA. *(Tries to make this a joke?)* Than all the shitty white women. Than all the –

I know this sounds super weird but just like,

DANA. Can you humor me

KJ. Are you being serious

DANA. You know how in my head I get, how neurotic I
am. My inner monologue is always [crazy!]

And sure those women are "my people," Technically.
I know that I'm [   ]. But they're really not. We have
a lot in common in some ways, but in other ways, in
Most ways, I'm So not like them, right?

Can we just make fun of them? Can you just tell me
that I'm – that I'm –

Oh god this is coming out so [wrong]

I'm sorry.

...

KJ. And then what

DANA. What

KJ. After you say sorry, then what

DANA. ...You tell me

Please, feel free to tell me

KJ. Feel free?

DANA. I didn't mean it like [that]

Can we start over

KJ. I don't think so

DANA. I'm such a fucking idiot

KJ. Stop

DANA. No really – I feel like a fucking idiot. I'm terrible

KJ. You're spiraling

DANA. And I know this is – [Fuck] – I know this is the
worst possible thing to do, like I've done all the reading

and I've listened to the podcasts and – oh god I sound like a parody don't I? I know I'm not supposed to wave that in your face but also like I promise you I have, I have done those things and read those [things] and I've seen the other women who [do this] and I'm not [them] I swear to god I know this is the Worst Possible Thing To Do but

(**DANA** *is crying.*)

KJ. Okay I'm gonna go

DANA. No no please. I'm trying – I'm Really trying to be a good person

I am a good person. I'm a good person.

Right KJ?

Right KJ?

Right KJ?

Right KJ /

KJ. You know I think I put people on a continuum.

Like on a continuum of, human behavior or, whatever. From "horrific" to "bad" and then "not that bad" and then "fine" and then "basically okay, sometimes." And everyone but the absolute worst makes the cut.

But lately I've been thinking: fuck the continuum. Why can't I be pickier? Not perfection, I don't need perfection but I do need – something, better

DANA. Come on KJ, it's me. It's just me. It's not [them.]

You know me. And I know you. Since we were eighteen, I know you so well. Come on, we've /

KJ. Do you

DANA. Do I what

KJ. Do you know me so well?

> (**DANA** *opens her mouth as if to try to answer.*)
>
> (*But finds that she can't.*)
>
> (**KJ** *considers* **DANA**.)
>
> (*Until pretty quickly, she does not.*)
>
> (*This monologue should have a stream-of-consciousness quality to it.*)
>
> (*As if* **KJ** *is walking down a long hallway and these thoughts are popping into her head, building off each other.*)

KJ. I've had two root canals and eight stiches.

Six sinus infections and fifteen migraines.

One panic attack, I think.

I'm fucking great at my job.

I'm fucking terrible at karaoke.

And sometimes I forget to recycle

And sometimes I forget to pee after sex and I give myself a UTI

And sometimes I'm really sad

And sometimes I wear this blue dress that has a little cut-out in the lower back and it makes me feel like I'm In My Body, like I'm Owning my body, which is kind of a relief because on certain days I feel like I'm hovering above myself somewhere on the ceiling.

I've seen every single rom-com from the early 2000s

Watched Kate Hudson and Katherine Heigl get messy and weepy and fall in love, and be adored for it

The audacity of white women to put their neuroses on display and make it cute

Couldn't stand it. Kept watching though.

I have allergies

I have anxiety

I have an immersion blender I do not know how to use

I have this jar where I keep all the times I almost let myself get angry but didn't

All the times I've really wanted to lose my shit,

But didn't.

I love my ankles

I love my collarbone

I love my brain

I forget birthdays

I got my period on my friend's expensive couch and lied to her face about it

I think I'm going to make a great caretaker for my parents someday

And I think I'm going to take a trip by myself somewhere, soon

Portugal, maybe? Berlin?

I don't know yet, I don't know. But I will. Yeah. I will.

DANA. I – I'm sorry, I don't understand

I thought – I thought you were going to say something else

I thought you were going to call me out. Or you know, "put me in my place." Or say something about, politics or

DANA. something

[   ]

KJ. The other day, when I walked home to my apartment, the sun was bouncing off the glass buildings in this way that reminded me of old photos of New York I'd seen as a kid. And there was a Mr. Softee truck on the corner even though it wasn't quite ice cream weather yet but this man thought he'd try, so he circled the block, that jingle playing on loop. And I stood there at the crosswalk, listening to it, that little *(She sings a tiny bit of it.*)*

And I could feel my heart pumping blood into my lungs and someone was on a date in a horse drawn carriage and a little kid was tugging on her mom's sleeve and she smiled at me and I smiled back and I wasn't invisible but I wasn't hyper-visible and no one was expecting anything of me or praising me or patronizing me or thanking me, thanking me, thanking me

I was just there. At the center of my own life.

I was right there.

DANA. Wait

KJ. I already left

(She did.)

(She's miles away.)

(Is she on a beach?)

DANA. No – no –

---

* A license to produce *53% Of* does not include a performance license for any third-party or copyrighted music. Licensees should create an original composition or use music in the public domain. For further information, please see the Music and Third-Party Materials Use Note on page iii.

Hello?

KJ, Hello?

> (**DANA** *is alone.*)

Ok so now – now, what

What should I [do.]

Am I –

I'm a good person

I'm a good person

> (*Losing steam.*)

I'm a good person

I'm a good person

I'm a good /

> (*Blackout.*)

End of Play

CITATIONS

In 2016, 53% of white women voted for Donald Trump.

Rogers, Katie. "White Women Helped Elect Donald Trump (Published 2016)." *The New York Times*, 10 Nov. 2016, www.nytimes.com/2016/12/01/us/politics/white-women-helped-elect-donald-trump.html.

In 2020, 55% of white women voted for Donald Trump.

"National Results 2020 President Exit Polls." *Cable News Network*, www.cnn.com/election/2020/exit-polls/president/national-results/21. Accessed 7 Feb. 2023.

56% of white women voted for Mitt Romney.

"Half of White Women Continue to Vote Republican. What's Wrong with Them? | Moira Donegan." *The Guardian*, 9 Nov. 2018, www.theguardian.com/commentisfree/2018/nov/09/white-women-vote-republican-why.

53% of white women voted for John McCain.

Nast, Condé. "What's up with White Women? They Voted for Romney, Too." *The New Yorker*, 8 Nov. 2012, www.newyorker.com/news/john-cassidy/whats-up-with-white-women-they-voted-for-romney-too. Accessed 7 Feb. 2023.

55% of white women voted for George W. Bush.

"CNN.com Election 2004." *Cable News Network*, www.cnn.com/ELECTION/2004/pages/results/states/US/P/00/epolls.0.html.

www.ingramcontent.com/pod-product-compliance
Lightning Source LLC
Chambersburg PA
CBHW070346120726
47909CB00008B/2743